DROO

First Published 1985

Ashton Scholastic Limited
165 Marua Road, Panmure, P O Box 12328, Auckland 6, New Zealand

Ashton Scholastic Pty Ltd
P O Box 579, Gosford, NSW 2250, Australia

Scholastic Inc.
730 Broadway, New York NY 10003, USA

Scholastic-TAB Publications Ltd
123 Newkirk Road, Richmond Hill, Ontario L4C 3G5, Canada

Scholastic Publications Ltd
9 Parade, Leamington Spa, Warwickshire CV32 4DG, England

Text copyright © Barbara Hill
Illustrations copyright © Rita Parkinson

National Library of New Zealand
Cataloguing-in-Publication data

HILL, Barbara.
    Droo / by Barbara Hill; illustrated by
Rita Parkinson. — Auckland, N.Z.: Ashton
Scholastic, 1985. — 1 v. — (Read by reading
series)
    Children's story.
    ISBN 0-908643-44-6
        428.6 (NZ823.2)
    1. Readers (Elementary). I. Parkinson, Rita.
II. Title. III. Series.

5432   78/8

Typesetting by Jacobsons Graphic Communications Group
Printed by Jacaranda Wiley (HK) Ltd, Hong Kong

DROO

by Barbara Hill

illustrated
by Rita Parkinson

READ BY READING Series

Ashton Scholastic

Auckland   Sydney   New York   London   Toronto

I know the Droo that's in the Zoo.
He's very nice. He's very blue.
My dear old, lonely Aunty Smeech
found him wandering on the beach.

She asked his name and he said, "Droo."
She told him, "I'll look after you.
Come and make your home with me.
I'd like a Droo for company."

7

The Droo said, "Right!" and home they went.
My Aunty thought him heaven sent —

until she asked what he would eat,
"Bones, or bread, or good, red meat?"
That's when the Droo, in certain tones,
cried, "Me! Eat meat and bread and bones?

"Now look Miss Smeech, get one thing straight . . .
that's the sort of food I hate!
You asked me here to live with you,
so give me food that's coloured *blue*."

Then round and round her house he went,
showing Aunty what he meant,
and when he saw the colour blue
he drooled and then began to chew.

He ate the flowers — they were blue.
He gobbled up the blue vase too.
He ate three towels, the blue bath mat,
he sniffed the soap and then ate that.

He ate the blue Delft china jug,
a table cloth, a fireside rug.

He ate twelve books, an antique cup . . .
if it was blue he ate it up.

"Stop, please stop!" poor Aunty cried.
But then the naughty Droo espied
the velvet drapes — yes, they were blue —
he dragged them down and ate them too.

The Droo complained the drapes were tough.
Aunty cried, "Now that's enough!"
But no! He ate the Wedgwood plate
and ambled off to try the gate.

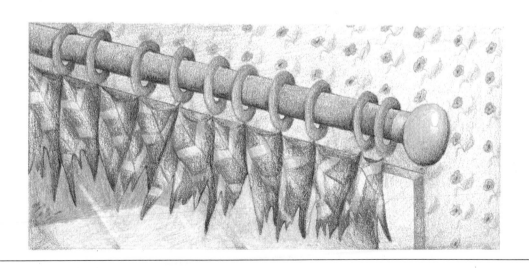

23

As Aunty then surveyed the mess,

back he came and eyed her dress.

This made my Aunty act at last.
She rang the Zoo, "Quick! Get here fast!
I've got a Droo that feasts on blue
and now he wants my sundress too."

"We're on our way," assured the man,
"I'm sending out our fastest van.
What a find — at last a Droo!
There's not another in the Zoo."

*　*　*

Droo now lives beside the Gled.
He's nice too, and very red.
And *everyone* asks Aunty Smeech
when next she's going to the beach.